The Red Priest

Dark Calling

Introduction

"Choosing to walk
through darkness to
protect the light, may
God guide my hand
to whom he wish to

smite, I see their evil I know their smell, I hear their name and send them back to hell, I live by faith and will die when called, for Gods will reigns over all". Why was I chosen? That's a question I could never answer, I was raised in the church but haven't been to one in years, heck, I didn't even raise my son in the church, yet it was Gods will for me to be his sword to vanquish evil on earth. I'm unaware if there are others out there like me, chosen to cleanse this world, all I know is the path I was chosen to walk and the city I was chosen to cleanse. My name is Jacob Craft, before a few months ago I was and average family man, with a wife Elizabeth Craft, and a five year old son Bryson Craft, living in Gridlock City. Things began to change when I started to have vivid dreams of and angel made of light coming to me and telling me of Gods plan for me, the dreams were confusing so I kept them to myself and brushed them off, until what I was told in the dreams started to come true. I was told by the angel that " I would see the face of the demon possessing its host, and that I would be able to track demons by their scent, lastly I would be able to hear a demons truth including their true name, and even though a demon is a creature of lies they would be unable to lie to me, their sins will be clear and after I vanquish them, their names will be carved into my flesh and their memories and power would become my own". It wasn't long after the dreams that I began to smell a foul odor that could only be described as evil, the smell was horrendous, and before long I was seeing the faces of demons everywhere I turned, it was frightening, to see how many demons live among us, my mission was clear, I had to kill these demons even if that meant one day I would become the very thing I was chosen to destroy. The only question is whether or not I'm crazy, because based on news reports and the FBI, I'm a serial killer.

Episode 1
The woman in red

Samatha Cain, she was my first, she was as pretty as an angel, with a heart as dark as the devils eyes, which I'm sure gleamed at the sight of her doing his works, oh how he must have cherished her, his agent of darkness. The news would later report on her as innocent little Sammy Cain, a wholesome girl next door, viciously slain in cold blood by a mad man, if they only knew, if they could only see what I saw when I looked at her. My day started off pretty normal, well as normal as it could considering I had come to the realization that I needed to kill someone, I struggle with that thought through breakfast with my family, smiling, acting as if I was listening to my wife talk, kissing my son on his forehead before he ran out to catch his school bus, auto pilot, that's the best way to describe it, I knew what I needed to do and yet I wanted a sign, any sign, to convince me not to. When I left for work I tried to distract myself from what I needed to do for God, by focusing on what I had to do for my family, I worked as a Gridlock Metro bus driver 8 hours a day 5 days a week, the pay was good, enough to take care of my family anyways, and it allowed me to be in constant contact with the people of my city, some of which I was able to build a rapport with, thinking back now, maybe that's why I was chosen, public transportation ran through the veins of the city allowing me to meet almost anyone on any given day. Samantha Cain got on my bus that day, wearing a white sundress with floral stitching and white heels, her sun kissed skin glowing as if she were a golden statue of a goddess, long blonde hair flowing from her head like a waterfall of light, and bright blue eyes as calming as floating in the middle of a cool blue swimming pool on a hot day, that's what she wanted me to see anyways, that's what she wanted everyone to see, but behind her veil, she was horrid, like a cloud briefly passing underneath the suns light blocking it momentarily, I was able to catch the quickest glimpse at Samantha's true face, her skin was clammy and grey with thick dark blue veins, her once athletic and curvy body was now emaciated and frail, her hair was the color of mud and looked as if it were damp, her eyes were missing and a white liquid was pouring out her eye sockets, whatever it was, it smelled, it smelled like spoiled milk and the sweet smell of rotting fruit, and like that, she returned to normal, when I heard her asking me how much the fare was. After taking her money she went to take her seat, and I knew she was the one. I continued on my route, watching her in my rearview and waiting to see what stop she would get off at, and after a few stops, she did, on West Greco Road, one of many shopping districts in the city, and where I would have to come and find her later. The rest of my day was clear, I felt a strange peace, those few hours were the first hours in a long time where I didn't see or smell any demons, as if my senses knew I already found my target and decided to give me a break, if only for a little while. After my shift ended I headed back to the bus terminal, clocked out and got in my car as usual but with one exception, normally I would head straight home, but today I had other business to take care of. West Greco Road, the sun barely in the sky, people trying to get home to their families, I found myself standing in the middle of a busy sidewalk looking for my needle in the haystack, I closed my eyes and took in the scent of the city, the smell of burning fuel from the traffic, the scent of greasy fast food from vendors and food trucks, colognes and perfumes from passersby, and the faint scent of Samantha Cain. It was in that instant I knew demons had unique scents, because I knew instantly that this particular scent was hers. I began to walk in the direction the scent was strongest,

the sun had all but
faded and darkness
began to fall on the
city, and with it came
a cold rain pouring
down as if to bury the
city, so heavy and
cold I could barely
breathe, and then, in
the distance I saw her.
Samantha Cain,
standing in the rain
by the curb just a few
blocks away, this was

perfect, I decided to head back to my car and drive over to her and offer her a ride. As I pulled up along side her I couldn't help but notice her cold dead stare, complete indifference to her surroundings, she was soaked, yet she stood there without a care in the world.

Jacob Craft; "hey need a ride?"

Samantha Cain; "no its fine, I'm actually waiting on a taxi"

Jacob Craft; "nonsense, its pouring out here hop in, its really no trouble at all"

Samantha Cain;
"are you sure?"

Jacob Craft; "yeah,
hop in"

Samantha Cain;
"thanks a bunch,
you're a life saver I'm
drenched"

Jacob Craft; "so where are you heading?"

Samantha Cain; "to work believe it or not, 2243 Graceland street"

Jacob Craft; "work at this time? Its getting pretty late"

Samantha Cain; "well I actually work at The Den, by day, but I also do some babysitting on the side, this job was kinda last minute"

Jacob Craft; "the Den? Is that the hair

salon on West Greco Road?"

   Samantha Cain; "well kinda, my boss would freak if I just let you call it a hair salon, its actually a requiem for the inner goddess in all women as my boss would say, but the best way to describe The Den is a one stop shop for the beautification of women, its a hair, nail, makeup and tanning salon, a spa and a female only gym"

Jacob Craft; "thats a mouth full, but yeah I think I heard about it, they also sell products by that Meisha girl right?"

Samantha Cain; "thats right, they don't just sell her products, The Den is her franchise, she has over two thousand store locations all over the world, Meisha Wolf is by far the most iconic and polarizing figure of this generation, you seem to know more then you let on"

Jacob Craft; "and you seem to take your job more seriously then you let on"

Samantha Cain; "not really, the jobs ok, but I'll admit I'm a huge Meisha Wolf fangirl"

Our conversation only lasted ten to twenty minutes, but it was enough of a distraction that she didn't even notice I was taking her in the complete opposite direction. An empty parking lot was as good a place as any, when I came to a stop we were parked in the center of the parking lot, thats when she started to pretend she was afraid.

Samantha Cain; "where are we? Whats going on?"

Jacob Craft; "drop the act demon, I

know what you are
and I'm here to kill
you"

She was such an
actress, shaking,
trying to imitate fear,
while trying to open
the passenger door.

Jacob Craft; "like I
said drop the act,
besides only I can
unlock your door,

you're trapped you
vile creature"

Samantha Cain;
"are you fucking
insane? What are you
talking about? If you
want money I can pay
just let me go"

Jacob Craft; "this is
Gods will, not my
own"

Samantha Cain;
"Gods will? Which
God? If this is the will
of a God then tell me
his name, who is my
accuser?"

Jacob Craft; "God is
God there is no
other"

Samantha Cain; "so you're just crazy, God is a title used to block people from seeking higher spiritual knowledge, your going to kill me using a generic term as your excuse?"

Jacob Craft; "blasphemy, your true nature is showing demon"

Samantha Cain; "demon? What kind? It seems you're just pulling ideas from cheesy horror movies, what real proof or information do you have?"

She was good,
funny how this girl
who worked at a hair
salon quickly became
a defense attorney,
but she couldn't fool
my nose, I could smell
her evil, she needed to
be killed and only I
could do it.

Jacob Craft; "you can't fool me so you might as well shut up"

Samantha Cain; "I can see in you're eyes you don't really wanna do this, you're struggling with this decision and you're trying your hardest to justify doing something insane"

Jacob Craft; "first law, now psychology? You're pretty clever"

Faith was all I had, she was right in a way, God was just a generic name, no one even knew where it originated, it was the same for terms like angel and demon. What was I supposed to do? Was I going crazy? Everything I knew to be true felt so real, but was it real because it was, or because I needed it to be? In the end it wouldn't matter, I pulled a hunting knife from my pocket that I had bought specifically for this moment, it was time for a leap of faith. I placed the hunting knife on the dashboard then unlocked the passenger door, and like a snake that could no longer hold back its fangs, Sammy Cain showed me her true nature, she could have ran like a

normal girl would
have, but instead she
grabbed the blade
and attempted to
plunge it into my
neck, I just barely was
able to block, but the
force was so great it
nearly broke my arm
doing so, the tip of the
blade even pierced
my skin, how could
she be human? Little
Sammy Cain, five

foot tall, eighty to ninety pounds, I was an athlete my whole life, wrestling, football, you name it I did it, even went to college on a football scholarship, yet this little girl almost over powered me, a six foot two inch tall man, weighing two hundred pounds. She was like a worker bee

in a way, because
after her first attack
she seemed to have
been drained, I could
literally feel the
tension leaving her
body as her arm
struggled to continue
to push the blade
passed my arm, her
face said it all, she
knew she blew her
shot, I reached for my
ball peen hammer as

she turned to run,
before she could fully
get out the car, I
struck her left knee as
hard as I could
considering the
cramped space, but it
was enough to get her
to fall to the ground,
as she struggled to
make it to her feet I
calmed myself, my
years as an athlete
taught me that over

excitement could quickly drain ones stamina, so I slowly walk over to her, and with my full strength this time struck her knee shattering it instantly, Gods wrath guided my hand, each strike positioned perfectly to break bones, ribs, tibias, radius and ulna, when I was done she was

like a jellyfish on land,
by this time the
internal bleeding was
visible all over her
body, so I grabbed
the hunting knife to
relieve some of the
swelling, just a few
cuts here and there
and she popped like a
water balloon, her
once white dress and
heels were now
painted red, before

she died I asked her one last time to confess, yet she never did. After getting in my car and heading home I couldn't help but feel a little doubt, after all, I was told demons wouldn't be able to lie to me, not to mention everything she said about my lack of knowledge of the God I claim to serve, then I heard her cell phone ring and realized she left her belongings in my car, after pulling over on the side of the road I reached into her bag and grabbed her cell phone, it had already stopped ringing but something told me it would be important, she had a finger print lock on it so I headed back to her body in order to unlock her phone, luckily no one had discovered her yet and I was able to quickly unlock her phone and reset her password, so much time had already passed so I couldn't check her phone right then and there, I needed to get home to my family. After I made it home I changed my clothes in the garage before going inside to explain why I was so late to my wife. Once again luck was on my side, my wife and son were both fast asleep, allowing me time to go through Samanthas phone. What I found painted a very clear picture of

Sammy Cains crimes, her bank records were off, for a girl who worked at a salon she had a little over a million dollars in savings, this was the first red flag, the second was her camera roll, image after image, video after video, were of children doing vile acts, the third flag was her messages and emails, her contact list was full of buyers who would pay her for the videos and images she would take of children she more than likely gained access to by babysitting, I couldn't help but become sick by the things I was seeing, I rush to the bathroom and began to vomit, after I

calmed down I
realized I had killed a
woman like it was
nothing yet now
because of these
images and videos I
was vomiting, thats
when I realized I
wasn't crazy, I didn't
kill a woman, I
destroyed a demon
which is why I felt no
remorse, I put her
belongings in the

trunk of my car then
went to lay down with
my wife, before long I
was sleep, and thats
when the angel
revealed to me, his
name was Lubelle,
and he was a Nag not
and angel which
didn't exist, and his
allegiance was to
Nazeerah who was
my great lord Nag,
not a god which was a

false title, he told me
my duty was to
destroy human vessels
for evil, people who
because of their
crimes become
beacons for Xinners
which are the true
name for demons, he
explained I would see
beyond their skin to
their dark and twisted
souls, and that their
crimes are what

create their scent and over time I would be able to distinguish between different crimes committed based on scent alone, I asked him why I was chosen and he explained it was my bloodline, one of my ancestors was what he called a Wardamor, a human with the power to transform

into a wolf, and
cursed to seek out an
destroy evil, my
Wardamor genes
were dormant leaving
me to weak to fight
Xinners, however
because of heightened
senses my dormant
Wardamor genes
would allow me to
track the evil in
humans, and that
over time using my

abilities would cause them to grow and awaken my inner Wardamor at a price, true Wardamor are forbidden to take human life no matter how vile, doing so causes them to instead of transforming into a wolf and having control of this form, they instead transform into humanoid wolf hybrids with no self control and a lust for blood and human flesh, known as Warloah, he told me I could learn more by seeking out artifacts known as pages of Brewl, and that within these artifacts was the knowledge of my ancestors as well as the histories of the heavens and hells.

When I woke up I felt so at peace, I knew I wasn't crazy, and I knew I needed to continue on this path, I got up to use the bathroom but almost as soon as I entered it I collapsed, my skin felt like it was on fire, I could feel something tearing away at my flesh, when I removed my shirt I could see

Samantha Cains
name being curved
into me, was this part
of being a Warloah?
For what looked like
something curved
with a knife it felt a lot
worse, as if I were
dying, I could feel
what Samantha felt as
I killed her, my bones
felt like they were
shattering and I could
feel how many times I

stabbed her, what did I get myself into? I guess hearing the commotion caused my wife to wake up, she rushed to the bathroom to check on me, there I was laying on the floor with a name curved into my skin, yet she didn't acknowledge it, she asked what was wrong and why I was on the floor but the name, it was like she couldn't see it. I struggled to my feet, trying to convince my wife that I was ok, but she was set on me going to the hospital, after a brief debate I was able to argue her down to me just staying home for the day, I made my way downstairs to the living room as she

went to make
breakfast, after sitting
down on the couch I
realize, maybe I did
need a day off, I
turned the tv on and
started flipping
through the channels,
and thats when I saw
him for the first time,
the detective that
would hunt me until
one of us was dead,

detective Nathan
Moorgraves.

To be continued…